SWITCH

Gecko Gladiator

Ali Sparkes

illustrated by
Ross Collins

OXFORD
UNIVERSITY PRESS

OXFORD
UNIVERSITY PRESS

Great Clarendon Street, Oxford OX2 6DP

Oxford University Press is a department of the University of Oxford.
It furthers the University's objective of excellence in research, scholarship,
and education by publishing worldwide in

Oxford   New York

Auckland   Cape Town   Dar es Salaam   Hong Kong   Karachi
Kuala Lumpur   Madrid   Melbourne   Mexico City   Nairobi
New Delhi   Shanghai   Taipei   Toronto

With offices in

Argentina   Austria   Brazil   Chile   Czech Republic   France   Greece
Guatemala   Hungary   Italy   Japan   Poland   Portugal   Singapore
South Korea   Switzerland   Thailand   Turkey   Ukraine   Vietnam

Oxford is a registered trade mark of Oxford University Press
in the UK and in certain other countries

British Library Cataloguing in Publication Data
Data available

ISBN: 978-0-19-2732392
1 3 5 7 9 10 8 6 4 2

Printed in Great Britain

Paper used in the production of this book is a natural,
recyclable product made from wood grown in sustainable forests.
The manufacturing process conforms to the environmental
regulations of the country of origin.

Photograph on page 127: Thanks to Tiny Drury, cool chameleon.

To Jacob James Harley Stewart
(who keps his socks on to read in bed)

With grateful thanks to
John Buckley and Tony Gent of
Amphibian and Reptile Conservation
for their hot-blooded guidance on
SWITCH's cold-blooded reptile heroes.

Danny and Josh
and Petty

Josh and Danny might be twins but they're NOT
the same. Josh loves getting his hands dirty and
learning about nature. Danny thinks Josh is a nerd.
Skateboarding and climbing are way cooler! And their
next door neighbour, Petty, is only interested in one
thing . . . her top secret SWITCH potion.

Danny

- FULL NAME: Danny Phillips
- AGE: 8 years
- HEIGHT: Taller than Josh
- FAVOURITE THING: Skateboarding
- WORST THING: Creepy-crawlies and tidying
- AMBITION: To be a stunt man

Josh

- **FULL NAME:** Josh Phillips
- **AGE:** 8 years
- **HEIGHT:** Taller than Danny
- **FAVOURITE THING:** Collecting insects
- **WORST THING:** Skateboarding
- **AMBITION:** To be an entomologist

Petty

- **FULL NAME:** Petty Hortense Potts
- **AGE:** None of your business
- **HEIGHT:** Head and shoulders above every other scientist
- **FAVOURITE THING:** SWITChing Josh & Danny
- **WORST THING:** Evil ex-friend Victor Crouch
- **AMBITION:** Adoration and recognition as the world's most genius scientist (and for the government to say sorry!)

CONTENTS

A Poxy Situation

'Do you think she's dead?'

Danny, wobbling on Josh's shoulders, peered through the dusty window into Petty Potts's front room. He didn't answer his twin brother but pressed his nose up hard against the glass, trying to see past the grimy net curtains and work out whether the large blue shape on the sofa was moving.

'Danny!' hissed Josh. 'You're breaking my back!' He was doubled up, supporting his brother's weight, and his forehead was grinding against the damp red brick under their neighbour's windowsill. 'Is she dead?!'

'It's hard to say,' muttered Danny. 'I mean— she never looks all that healthy at the best of times, does she?'

'No—but she doesn't usually look like a corpse!' grunted Josh. 'Is she moving?'

Danny got up onto his feet, treading carefully on each of his brother's shoulder blades, hanging on to Petty's rather rotten window frame. The top panes didn't have nets, so they'd be easier to see through.

'I can't hold you up any longer!' gurgled Josh, but he didn't have to. Three seconds later there was a creak and a crack and a crash and Danny had fallen through the window.

'Gah!' remarked Josh, in surprise. He stood up and glanced all around, guiltily. Had anybody seen his brother accidentally breaking and entering? No . . . there was nobody around. 'Danny! Are you OK!' he whispered, peering inside through the broken glass and wood. Below he could make out Danny, struggling out of a dusty grey net curtain, spluttering.

'OK—I'm coming in!' Josh said, carefully climbing through. It was a good thing really that the wooden frame had been weak, even if it meant that Petty's window had been smashed. If they'd broken down her front door they would probably be skewered on the end of poison-dipped spears by now or reduced to a heap of ash and charred bones or something. Petty had put some formidable defences in place in her house recently, but amazingly had failed to secure the window.

Danny had escaped the dusty net curtain by the time Josh jumped down next to him—and he wasn't cut by broken glass. That was good news. On the other hand, Petty was still motionless on the sofa. That was not so good. They looked at each other, gulping.

From this angle they could only see her grey mop of hair. It was hard to tell whether she was dead or alive. As he got closer Danny could see one small patch of wrinkled cheek. He prodded it, gingerly, with one finger. 'It's warm!' he said, with relief. And then he shrieked as Petty's hand suddenly swiped up and grabbed his wrist.

There was a moment of silence during which Petty eased herself up on one elbow and peered at him. 'Hello, Danny,' she croaked. 'Hello, Josh. What, exactly, are you doing in my front parlour?'

'We came to find out if you were still alive,' Danny said, panting with relief. 'You haven't been answering the door for days and we thought you might have died.'

'Oh really?' Petty raised an eyebrow behind her smeary spectacles.

'Well, you know . . . you are quite old,' Danny said.

'Danny!' Josh kicked his brother's ankle. 'Don't be rude!'

'No—not a bit of it!' Petty said, sitting up properly now. 'After all, I am ancient. It's a wonder

I can even walk, talk or safely visit the toilet. My heart could pop. I could just keel over at any time. Just one loud noise or a funny smell and it could be curtains for Old Granny Potts. Better not stand too close to me when you've got an attack of flatulence, Danny. You could take us both out.'

'So—why didn't you answer our calls? Our knocks? Our doorbell ringing?' enquired Josh.

'I have had chickenpox,' Petty said. And now that they looked properly they could see that she had a rash of rather nasty red pimples—many of them topped with a little yellow crust. 'I've been dreadfully tired and sore and I didn't feel like talking to anyone—or infecting anyone!'

Josh and Danny took a step back.

'Oh don't fret now!' Petty said. 'I'm not infectious any more. Once the spots get all scabby you're past the point of infecting anyone.'

'Phew,' sighed Danny, sinking into a worn leather armchair opposite Petty's couch. 'We thought it was all over for the SWITCH project.'

'I'm touched by your concern,' Petty said. 'But now that you're here, I might as well get out the chocolate cake. And then you can tell me about . . . this!' She dug in her pocket and held out something small, round and shiny.

'Our marble!' breathed Josh. 'Yes—and—well, you might want to look at these too.' He dug in his own pocket and withdrew a small black drawstring bag. In it were two marbles. One blue and one red. 'These two are like the green one you've got there. They have code in them and a hologram—just like your BUGSWITCH and REPTOSWITCH cubes.'

Petty stared at the marbles in Josh's palm as if she was desperately trying to remember something. After thirty seconds she got unsteadily to her feet. 'No—no good!' she snapped. 'Until I have chocolate cake and a large mug of tea not a single synapse is going to fire!'

'She means her brain isn't working,' muttered Josh to Danny, following Petty into the kitchen. 'Sit down, Petty. We'll get it,' he said, feeling guilty because she really did look pretty ropey. She was pale under the pox. He and Danny put the kettle on and got the cake out of a tin in the fridge while Petty sat at the table, rolling the three coded marbles around in her hand.

Soon they were all munching cake with thick chocolate icing and gulping down hot brown tea between mouthfuls. Petty's colour began to improve. The glimmer returned to her eyes as she continued to stare closely at the marbles.

'So,' she said, eventually. 'Where did these come from?'

Josh and Danny looked at each other and then back at Petty. 'We were hoping you could tell us that,' Josh said. 'They've been sent to *us*—by the Mystery Marble Sender. One at a time across the last three weeks or so. We thought maybe it was you.'

'Why on earth would it be *me*?' Petty asked.

'Well . . . because they've got code in them and a hologram,' explained Josh. 'Just like in your SWITCH cubes! We didn't think anybody else could make Serum Which Instigates Total Cellular Hijack.'

'And nobody else can!' agreed Petty. 'I made these, yes—I told you! But I can't remember when. Or why. Or what for. Remember, that nasty bag of bones Victor Crouch burnt out my memory after he tried to steal my SWITCH project work and claim it as his own! There are big echoing chambers of my brain with VACANT signs hung over them, thanks to my backstabbing former best friend.'

'Well . . . maybe Victor Crouch *did* manage to steal some of your formula after all—this bit,' Danny said.

'It looks like a SWITCH code for mammals,' Josh said. 'We had a look with my microscope and there's a bat shape in the blue one, and a cat shape in the red one.'

19

'There's a wolf shape in the green one,' Petty said. 'I started on insects with BUGSWITCH then rediscovered amphibians and reptiles after you helped me find the missing cubes containing the code to REPTOSWITCH. If I had been working in any kind of order the next thing I would have created would certainly have been MAMMALSWITCH.' She smiled. 'I really am fabulously good! Top calibre genius!'

'But who sent these to us?' insisted Josh. 'If it wasn't you.'

'Well why would it be me, you twaddlehead?' Petty said. 'Why would I exclude you from a brand new exciting SWITCH phase? And then send you vital parts of it, anonymously? You and Danny are my assistants. I need your help. And when the SWITCH formulae are all finally perfected you will join me upon the world's stage as the assistants of the GREATEST GENIUS SCIENTIST IN THE HISTORY OF MANKIND!!!' This last she said as an echoing shout, rising to her feet and raising her chocolate-y hands as if she was already on a stage being cheered by thousands of other less clever scientists.

'She's so modest,' muttered Danny.

'Hmmm . . .' Petty sank back down onto her kitchen chair and cut herself a second slice of cake. 'Did this Mystery Marble Sender include a note with the other marbles?'

'Yes—a note always comes first,' Josh said. 'With a clue to find the next marble.' He put several bits of paper with spiky handwriting on them into Petty's hand. 'So far we've found one marble in a barn owl's nest, one up in a light in the school hall and one—last week—in a ruined sea fort.'

'Whoever it is,' Danny said, 'they're spying on us and following us around. They even followed us on holiday!'

'Or they were following *me*,' Petty said, scanning the notes. 'Remember I was at your holiday beach too. Far more likely it's all about me . . .'

'Even though they were all addressed to us?' snorted Josh.

'That's just to throw me off the scent,' murmured Petty. 'It's all about me.'

'So modest,' muttered Danny.

'I'm going to have to pack up my lab and go even sooner than I thought,' Petty said, slapping the notes down on the table. 'First the attempted break-in—now notes to you which are clearly meant for ME! It's getting more dangerous here by the minute!'

'But—where will you go?' asked Josh, appalled. 'And . . . what about the rest of the REPTOSWITCH project. You were going to SWITCH us into snakes and—and—'

'Alligators!' continued Danny, forlornly biting into his second slice of cake. 'Fwee fwant koo be falligators!'

'Don't talk with your mouth full,' chided Petty. 'And don't be so selfish! Can't you see? They're closing in! If my lab gets discovered I'll be kidnapped and tortured for all my secrets! And so, very possibly, will you! I don't think it's safe for you to come round here and see me any more.'

'What?' Danny stood up. 'After all we've done for you! You're just going to chuck us off the SWITCH project?'

'Don't be so melodramatic, Danny!' Petty stood up too. 'I mean I think you'll have to meet me somewhere else . . . in my new secret lab!'

'Your new lab? Is it ready?' Josh asked.

'Very nearly,' Petty said. 'In fact . . . I will let you see it tomorrow. Take this.' She dug into her other pocket and then handed Josh a small white spray bottle with a big G written on it in marker pen. 'It will allow you to find your way in. Do NOT use it before you reach the new address. Josh—I'm trusting you not to let Danny persuade you before then.'

'Oi!' Danny said, looking wounded.

'Only when you get there!' went on Petty. 'Or I won't trust you again. And make sure you're not followed.'

Josh grasped the SWITCH spray bottle, a surge of deep excitement running through him. 'Which SWITCH is it?' he breathed.

'You'll find out soon enough,' Petty said. 'Meet me here . . .' she handed Danny a scrap of paper with an address written on it. '. . . at 2 p.m. tomorrow.'

'Here?' Danny said, puzzled.

'All will become clear,' Petty said, affecting what she obviously thought was a mysterious expression, but looking really more as if she had a bad case of wind. 'Now—off you go. Unless you want to help me apply bicarbonate of soda to my pustules . . .'

Princessland

'Oh no,' Danny said. 'Oh no, oh no, oh no!'

'Errm,' added Josh.

This was worse than they had imagined. Far worse.

The brothers stood, frozen, in front of a large warehouse-style shop. It was located in a superstore park about twenty minutes' walk from their house. Mum and Dad thought they'd gone up to the recreation ground. They would be amazed if they saw where their sons really were at this moment. Standing outside PRINCESSLAND.

'This has got to be a mistake!' Danny peered at the address on the note again, but no—the unit number above the door of Princessland was unmistakably 18. Danny had been surprised enough when Petty had written down Unit 18,

RAINBOW BUSINESS PARK—but this? 'This can't be right,' he went on. 'She's a genius scientist! She should be building her lab in a hollowed out extinct volcano!'

'Not many of those around here,' pointed out Josh.

'All right then—a disused water tower. An abandoned nuclear waste dump—I don't know. Anything but this!' Danny's voice wobbled as he stared up again at Princessland. It was a shop filled with lovely things for lovely girls. Dresses and shoes and tiaras and tie-on fairy wings and dollies and little shiny handbags and strawberry flavoured lip gloss and . . .

'Face it,' Josh said. 'Petty Potts has gone to Princessland.' It sounded a bit like a kind way of saying someone had died or gone mad . . . and as far as Danny was concerned it was much the same.

'I'm not walking in there!' he said. 'Let's use the SWITCH spray and go inside in disguise.'

'No,' Josh said. 'For one thing, we don't know what we're going to turn into, do we? G could stand for anything in the reptile world . . . It could be a Gila Monster. Half a metre long with a venomous bite. Or a Galapagos tortoise—way too slow to get away before the RSPCA shows up. And for another thing—read that!'

There was a note at the bottom of the address. It read: 'Go to the lobby at the back and SWITCH to get in under the red door. BEWARE! NOBODY MUST SEE! Keep a low profile.'

'Keep a low profile?' spluttered Danny. 'In Princessland, when we're *boys*? Is she nuts?'

Josh shrugged. There was no need to answer that one. He grabbed Danny's arm. 'Come on. If we stand out here much longer we'll attract attention. Just walk in. We can pretend we're buying a birthday present for our sister.'

'Jenny's fourteen. I think she's grown out of fairy wings!' Danny hissed.

'We can pretend she's four,' Josh said.

Inside Princessland it was every bit as bad as Danny had feared. As soon as they stepped through the door three sparkly fairies on springs bounced down into their faces, cooing in American accents: 'Hi there, best friend!' and 'The fairies love YOU!' and 'Let's go shopping in the Fairyland mall!' Danny screamed and swatted them away as if he was being attacked by wasps. Wasps styled by Disney.

Danny ducked away and nearly cannoned into a big whiteboard with PARTY TIME! written on it in glittery purple pen. 'Princessland welcomes Princess Megan and all her friends to a DAMSELS PARTY at 4 p.m. today!'

'I mean—what does that even *mean*?' he found himself musing. 'Does anyone really know what a damsel is?'

'It's a kind of princess, I think,' Josh said. 'Usually in distress. And they seem to wear cone-y things with ribbons on their heads . . .'

'You know too much,' muttered Danny, darkly.

He shuddered and turned to look at the large shop floor. It was festooned in glittering pink, yellow, and purple displays of girly stuff. There were huge screens dangling from the ceiling all around the store, playing endless Chatz TV sponsored adverts for all the girly toys available, with non-stop tinkly music. Even the Darcy Show was getting in on the act. Mum and Jenny's favourite talk show presenter, wearing her trademark yellow jacket and black sequinned trousers, was gushing about her own tiny doll—

the Diddly DeeDee—one minute and then her own brand of toy microphone the next. A rack of sparkly yellow My Little Microphones stood to their left, just behind the attack fairies. Danny and Josh stared past it, trying to work out the quickest route to the red door that Petty had mentioned. It was clear they would have to cross all the way to the back of the store.

'Have we really got to do this?' Danny wailed.

Josh grabbed his arm again. 'Stop freaking out!' he snapped. 'Remember! Low profile!'

But Danny's fight with the fairies had already attracted attention. At least six girls were now peering at them, all in giggling pair formation, while one small girl and her mother just glanced at them with disdain and then hastened around a corner. Josh dragged Danny along the Diddly DeeDee aisle—its tall shelves packed with tiny pink dolls and a phenomenal amount of clothes and accessories, most of which could fit into a matchbox. 'Why do they have to be so yellow and purple and pink?' Danny murmured. 'Why are girls so nuts about pink? PINK!'

'Just don't look,' Josh advised his brother, as Danny's eyes started to get fixed. 'Now—you see the My Tiny Horsey rotating display? We've got to get to the far side of that . . .'

'My Tiny Horsey?' whimpered Danny, his eyes going glassy. He'd seen the adverts for My Tiny Horsey on TV. My Tiny Horsey had eyelashes and necklaces and manes and tails of different colours and you could put special glittery nail polish on its hooves . . .

'Snap out of it!' hissed Josh, whacking Danny on the back of the head. 'It's just girls' toys! Pretend they're all called DEATHKILL STALLION and they're black and grey and carrying machine guns and you'll be OK!'

Danny did his best and despite some giggling very close behind him, and a definite whiff of glittery hoof polish, he got to the far side of the display alongside Josh. Here they nearly collided with the mother and daughter who had scurried away from them earlier. Both wore identical long lumpy dark coats, even though it was quite warm outside. And both of them had identical curly brown hair and grey eyes which they narrowed suspiciously at Josh and Danny. The girl was not much older than Josh and Danny but she looked as disapproving as her mother as they stalked away, wrapping their coats tightly around them.

'I thought they were going to start hissing at us for a moment there,' Danny said. 'What's their problem?'

'Never mind,' breathed Josh, tugging Danny across to the lobby area. 'We've made it.'

'Aaaargh!' shrieked Danny. He had inadvertently snagged a pair of pink and gold fairy wings on his shoulder as he'd run through the dressing up aisle. 'GETITOFFMEEE!' he wailed and Josh, with a weary sigh, removed the wings as if they were a large moth. He nipped back into the aisle and hung them up on the fairy dressing up display. 'Take home a Diddly DeeDee today,' urged the Darcy Show presenter from a nearby screen. 'She's just like me . . . only Diddly Deeee!'

Josh ran away.

'Come on—look—there's the red door,' he said, as soon as he got back. And there it was, tucked out of sight around the corner from the shop floor. Next to it was a blue door with a PRIVATE sign on it. On the red door there was just one small paper sign taped into place. It read MUTATIO INC.

'Mutatio?' Danny whispered. 'What's that got to do with Petty Potts?'

'It's Latin,' Josh said. 'I think it means change or . . . switch.' Josh had picked up quite a bit of Latin because of all the Latin names of wildlife he'd read about.

He tried the door. It was locked. Of course, he'd known it would be. Why would they need to SWITCH if they could just walk in? He got out the spray bottle and glanced around. Nobody was anywhere near them and they were tucked out of sight of the main store. Despite all the fuss Danny had made there was no sign of any member of staff coming. 'Come on,' he said. 'Let's SWITCH.'

He sprayed them both and a few seconds later the red door shot up to the size of a house as he and Danny shrank down to their new shape and size. The crack under the door now looked like the gap you'd find beneath a bench. Easy to get under.

'Oh-ho-hoho!' marvelled Danny, staring at his brother. 'That is really cool!'

There was a metal kick plate at the foot of the red door which mirrored back Josh's image. He turned, on four feet, to see what he had become. 'Wow! I'm a gecko!' Josh breathed. He checked the underside of his feet. 'A Tokay gecko! WOW!'

He was a magnificent sight. A neat, sleek lizard covered in fabulous fine yellow scales with orange and blue spots. His belly was a pale milk white and his face was lit up by two dark, glinting, orb-like eyes. His snout was rounded, with a wide smiling mouth. His feet were dainty. Their five toes had squishy pads on them which made them look

like the petals on a flower. Josh knew these 'petals'
were one of the most amazing things about his
new form—he couldn't wait to find out if they
really worked. Turning, he checked out his tail. It
was long and leaf shaped, tapering to a neat point.

'Oh great,' Danny said, also staring into the
metal mirror. 'Oh—just great!'

Danny was much like Josh in shape and size,
from his big eyes and petal shaped toes to his tail.

But there were two differences.

He was stripy.

And he was pink.

Pretty in Pink

Josh laughed so hard he thought his inner gecko workings might burst. 'But, Danny . . .' he spluttered, between a series of high pitched chirrups and clicks, 'you're so pretty!'

Danny smacked Josh in the face with his tail and scurried under the door. On the other side there was a cliff of concrete. Followed by another cliff of concrete. And then another. A staircase.

Josh arrived at his side, still shaking with laughter. He opened his mouth to say something but Danny gave him a fierce stare. 'DON'T!' was all he said and Josh bit down on his next joke. After all Danny's freaking out about the pink and glittery stuff in the shop, he could have been designed by Princessland.

Of course, Josh was a very pretty gecko too—but the orange and blue spots weren't at all girly. Why they'd both SWITCHed with such different colours Josh couldn't say. Maybe it was just Danny's inner pinkness coming out.

'So,' Danny said, pinkly. 'What's going to eat us today?'

'We're not in much danger here,' grinned Josh. 'Unless Petty's bought herself a cat. Come on—I've got something to show you!' And Josh ran up the step. Literally—up it. He didn't even have to try to work out how to reach the first ledge and haul himself up—he ran up the smooth concrete without any difficulty at all.

'Whoa! Let me try!' Danny said, following his brother. He'd been climbing as a lizard before, but that had been up a tree with lots of easy claw-holds to help. This surface was completely flat and smooth. As a sand lizard he would have struggled—but as a gecko . . . no problem!

Ahead of him, Josh wasn't bothering with the stairs at all—he was just scampering up the wall of the stairwell, heading for the ceiling in a straight line. He was letting out little squeaks and clicks of excitement which echoed off the hard plastered walls. 'You see these?' He lifted one foot and showed off its toes. Underneath each toe was a group of tiny white mushroom-like things. 'They're called setae!' chirruped Josh. 'They stick like glue every time we press them against the wall—they're incredibly strong! But then they just pop off again when we want to carry on. Scientists all over the world have been trying to make something that does what a gecko's foot does! I was reading about it just last week!'

Danny caught up with his brother. He'd forgotten his unfortunate colour now and was hugely enjoying the climb. 'We're like Spiderman!' he marvelled.

'Yeah—except that Spiderman is pretend—and geckos do it for real!' Josh grinned at his brother in delight, revealing a row of small, sharp teeth. 'Now watch this!' And he ran right up to the top of the wall and effortlessly flipped his lizardy body upside down before walking jauntily across the ceiling. 'Whoooo-hooo! Look at meeee!' he called.

Danny wasted no time in following him. Walking upside down on the ceiling was amazing . . . although he and Josh had done it once before. 'We did this when we were flies, remember?' he said.

'Yeah . . . and that was cool too,' Josh said. 'But now we're doing it with grace and style. We're not just about to go and vomit all over someone's cake mix, are we? This time we're beautiful!'

'And we can't get eaten by a spider,' added Danny, happily.

'Nope . . . we eat the spider!' Josh said. 'Fancy a snack?' And he ran towards the corner of the stairwell ceiling where a few spindly cellar spiders hung in fine strands of web. As soon as they saw him they began to swing around wildly, hoping to put him off them by seeming bigger than they were through the wild, blurry movement. Josh was very tempted to snap one up—his lizard instinct was telling him to have some munchies right here, right now.

But he was soft hearted. He remembered how it felt to be a spider about to be eaten. He couldn't do it. 'Come on, Danny,' he said, turning away from the arachnid snack counter. 'Let's go and find Petty.'

'OK,' Danny said. Three legs were poking out of his mouth.

'You didn't!'

'Didn't what?' asked Danny, innocently, with a gulp.

'Never mind,' chuckled Josh. He knew Danny would have blocked out all memory of his little snack already. Josh ran back to the wall and down to another door. At the foot of the door a greenish light was shafting through. He headed for it and slipped under the crack easily. Danny arrived beside him a few seconds later.

They were in a large room under sloping eaves. The loft area, Danny guessed. It was huge at the moment, of course, because they were small lizards—but even as humans it would be pretty big. Three high windows along one side, and slanting windows in the ceiling above them, would normally let in plenty of light, but they were all covered in dark blinds and the room was bathed in the green glow of a bank of Petty's computer monitors along a high bench. Josh and Danny wandered across the wooden floor, staring all around them. The room was clearly a laboratory—much bigger than the one beneath Petty's garden shed. Its many shelves and tables were filled with bottles and boxes and Bunsen burners and test tubes and weird gadgets of every kind. A large mouse cage took up one corner. And in the centre was a familiar square tent of plastic— the SWITCHing chamber.

'Well,' Petty said, stepping out of the chamber and peering down at them in the dim light. 'What do you think?'

Bang to Wrongs

Josh and Danny told her how impressed
they were—but all that came out were those
chirruping, clicking, and occasionally grunting
noises.

'Aaah—geckos! The noisiest lizards there are!'
Petty said, smiling at them appreciatively. 'The
only reptiles which can make noises audible to
humans, don't you know? Well—one of you *is* a
pretty boy!' she added, kneeling down and patting
Danny on the head. He growled.

'But I need you to SWITCH back now so we
can talk,' Petty said. And she swiftly squirted them
with a bottle of antidote spray.

'Aa-aaw!' Josh was disappointed. 'I wanted to
walk across your ceiling!'

'Plenty of time for that later,' Petty said.

'How come he got to be all cool with spots and I turned into Barbie Gecko?' snapped Danny, folding his arms huffily.

'Well, you're very much the same—it's just a skin pigment issue,' Petty said. 'Although it does suggest that the formula is a little unstable . . . again.' She looked slightly concerned.

'Unstable? That'll be the third unstable SWITCH you've let us try!' squeaked Danny. 'Have you ever heard of Health and Safety?'

'The second,' corrected Petty. 'I didn't let you try the TurtleSWITCH, you may recall. You stole it and tried it entirely of your own free will!'

'But the Chameleon one was unstable too,' argued Danny. 'And you let us try that even when your mouse ended up half rodent, half chameleon!'

'I don't know why you fuss so,' Petty said. 'You're always fine in the end. Cutting edge science can't be perfectly safe. I am a genius and I must push the boundaries.'

'Hmmm,' Danny muttered. 'Funny how you always push the boundaries from a safe distance! I've never seen *you* try the SWITCH out!'

'I'm much older than you. My bones are far too brittle,' Petty said with a dismissive wave. 'Anyway—enough of all this. I wanted you to see my new lab—and here it is!'

'Why have it over Princessland?' Josh asked. 'Are you trying to mess with our minds?'

'What did you expect? A hollowed out extinct volcano? I am now based here because it is the very last place that government spies would think of looking for me,' explained Petty. 'And if they see me coming into the store they'll think I've just come to buy something pretty for a . . . niece or something.'

Josh and Danny stared at Petty. They could not imagine her ever buying something from Princessland.

Petty held up a glittery pink bag carrying the store's name. 'See!' she said. 'I always carry one of these out with me when I go.'

'What's in it?' Josh asked.

'Screwed up tissues, dried calamine lotion and chickenpox scabs mostly,' Petty said, peering into the bag.

There was a short silence and then a further pause while Josh and Danny massaged the rigid masks of horror off their faces.

'Come on, come on—over here!' Petty said, and led them to a corner of the room where a microscope and several jars and boxes lay in a pool of white light from a desk lamp. 'I've been studying the marbles and you're right—all three of them do contain code for MAMMALSWITCH. I recognize my own brilliant work! I must have made the formula . . . maybe years ago while I was still working for the government. And there are six marbles, the same way there were six BUGSWITCH cubes and six REPTOSWITCH cubes.'

'How do you know there are six?' Josh asked.

'Because, when I was clearing out the shelves of my old lab I found this,' Petty said. She held up a small box, covered in blue velvet. It looked much like the square red and green velvet boxes which contained the BUG and REPTILE SWITCH cubes—but this box was round. Inside there was a ripple of some silky blue material across six round dents. In three of these Petty had pressed the first three marbles—red, green and blue—but the other three dents were empty.

'So . . . did you hide the marbles, the same way you hid the REPTOSWITCH cubes?' Danny asked. 'In case Victor Crouch double-crossed you and came looking for them?'

'I don't know,' sighed Petty. 'Obviously that bit of memory is burnt out, or I would have thought to ask you to look for these when I asked you to look for the REPTOSWITCH cubes in the summer. And anyway . . . if I did hide them, somebody else has clearly found them. Or more likely stolen them.'

'Who?' Josh asked. 'Victor Crouch again?'

Petty reached behind her and took down a wooden frame. In it, much to their amazement, was a photo of Victor Crouch. He was wearing a black hat and waving cheerily at the photographer, the one spiky black fingernail on his little finger pointing up into the air. Had he possessed any, his eyebrows would have been raised. But as peculiar as Petty's old nemesis looked, it was something else which made them gasp—he had his arm around none other than Petty Potts.

'Yes,' sighed Petty. 'This was when we were friends . . . or so I thought.'

The Petty in the photo looked as much as ten years younger. Her hair was darker and she had one or two fewer chins—and those chins were definitely less whiskery. Someone else's hand was tucked through the crook of Petty's left arm, but they were cropped out of the picture.

'This was taken while we were working together in the secret government laboratories,' remembered Petty. 'Little did I know that only a year or so later he would have framed me in a very different way! And lost me my job and tried to steal all my genius work! I found this also while I was clearing out the old lab. I keep it to remind me never to trust anyone! You hear me, boys?' Her voice became shrill as she started bashing the picture against the wall. 'Never trust ANYONE! NEVER, NEVER, NEVER!!!' There was a tinkle of broken glass.

'O . . . K,' Josh said, stepping away. 'So . . . no other ideas about who the Mystery Marble Sender is?'

'Nope,' snapped Petty. 'Were there postmarks on any of the letters?'

'Only on one parcel,' Danny said. 'All the others were hand delivered—apart from one which came on a parachute. The parcel had a London postmark. It was a set of books Josh had won in a wildlife competition with Chatz TV. A clue was tucked in with it.'

'London . . . hmmm. Well, that's not much help,' grunted Petty. She slapped the broken picture frame face down on her workbench. 'No idea at all! And even LESS idea why this Mystery Marble Sender is sending them to YOU two. Go on—go on home now and see if there have been any more clues! Keep watch! Never rest! Watch from behind your curtains at ALL TIMES! If you watch all the time, sooner or later the Mystery Marble Sender will slip up and you'll SEE him!'

'Fine,' Danny said, grabbing Josh's arm. 'We'll go now.'

He and Josh left Petty shouting at the broken picture frame and let themselves out. The door at the foot of the stairs had a deadlock which they could open from the inside, so they got back out into the lobby and then left it to fall shut behind them. The only way back in would be if Petty opened it—or they SWITCHed again.

'Watch from behind our curtains at all times!' scoffed Danny. 'What does she think we are—MI5 spies? Doesn't she know we have to go to school? And bed?'

'She's going a bit wrong,' Josh said. He rubbed his nose and looked worried. 'I thought she might if we told her about the marbles.'

'Hey—she's lost her marbles!' quipped Danny, but Josh gave him a stony look. 'OK, I'll shut up,' Danny sighed.

They stepped out into Princessland, trying to act normal again. Or more normal than last time. And then a series of things happened very fast.

First Josh was knocked over as somebody ran past him. Then someone else tripped over him, cursing loudly, and then a large coat was shoved in his face and then a loud alarm went off.

Danny, who'd gone ahead, trying to avoid looking at the fairy outfits, was spun around by the impact of someone bashing into his shoulder. It was the woman in the long coat, running past him. Her daughter, who wasn't wearing a long coat any more, was pulling stuff out of her jumper and chucking it on the floor as she skidded after her mother, bawling 'Maa! Maaa! Wait for meeeee!'

Danny ran over to Josh, who was struggling out from under the coat. Just as his surprised face

emerged there was a shout. 'OY! You two! STOP
RIGHT THERE!' And a heavy hand landed on
Danny's shoulder.

'SO! You think nicking stuff from Princessland
is a larf, do you?' said the voice. Danny looked up,
shocked, into the face of a burly security guard.
'Well, sunshine, I'm calling the police . . . and you
two . . .' The guard dragged Josh up by his collar,
'. . . are coming with ME!'

Desperate Diddlies

Josh and Danny were dragged along by their
elbows through the shop, loudly protesting their
innocence. The store manager, a thin, nervous
looking man in a pale pink shirt, hurried behind
them carrying the dumped coat and all the things
which had dropped out of it. They all arrived
in a small square office with two-way-mirror
windows, a desk and three chairs. On the wall
was a sign which read "WE ALWAYS PROSECUTE
SHOPLIFTERS!" The guard shoved them across the
room and pulled the door shut while the manager
smacked a button on the wall which silenced the
ringing alarm.

'Right!' snapped the security guard, who wore a
grey uniform, a peaked cap and a look of righteous
menace across his rather square face. 'So . . . let's

see what we have here, shall we?' He took the coat and the things bundled up with it and began slapping them all, one by one, onto the desk. 'ONE—Diddly DeeDee double doll set. TWO—Diddly DeeDee fashion boots set. THREE—Diddly DeeDee doggy kennel including Diddly Doggy and DiddlyDoggy Dinner Dish.'

Danny let out a snort of laughter. He just couldn't help it. The security guard's large, sausage thick fingers paused, just as they were about to pluck yet another Diddly DeeDee treat from the coat. 'You think this is funny, do you, boy? You thinking diddling us out of Diddly DeeDees is just a joke do you?'

Danny snorted again, Josh bit his lip, and then they both just exploded into gales of laughter.

'Have it your way!' snarled the security guard, emptying another ten or twelve packets of Princessland goodies all over the desk, including three yellow toy microphones. 'Let's see what the police have to say about this, shall we? Mr Butch— please call the police!'

'Erm—I'll have to call from the manager's office,' Mr Butch said. 'You'd better come with me to verify what's happened . . .'

'Fine—we'll lock these two young thieves in here until they arrive!' the security guard said. And then he and the manager went out and slammed the door shut, locking it firmly behind them.

'Oh diddly dear,' gurgled Danny, wiping away tears.

Josh got control. 'This is not good, Danny! This is really not good. What will Mum and Dad say when we get arrested? For shoplifting?!'

'We're innocent!' repeated Danny. 'They'll believe us! And there must be security cameras or something, where we can show them the real shoplifters!'

'But . . . Mum and Dad will want to know why we were here,' pointed out Josh.

Danny's face went serious. 'Oh no . . .' he moaned. 'What if people we know find out that we were in Princessland? We'll have to move house! Leave town!'

'There's only one thing for it,' Josh said. 'We've got to escape before they make us tell them our names and addresses.' He pulled the bottle of GeckoSWITCH out of his pocket. 'And this is how!'

Danny jumped to his feet. 'Spray me! NOW!'

When the security guard and Mr Butch came back, ready to tell the two young criminals that the police were on their way, they were shocked into silence. As soon as they unlocked the door and stepped into the tiny office they could see the inmates had vanished. Completely.

'Whaaa-aaa-aaa?' queried the security guard. Beside him, Mr Butch just stood with his mouth opening and closing and no sound coming out. They checked under the desk. In a cupboard. Even behind some coats which hung from hooks on the wall.

'But—but—but . . . how?' spluttered the security guard, his eyes bulging with disbelief. 'We locked them in! And that's a proper deadlock, that is! And there's no window to the outside . . . and no way they could have gone through the floor . . . it's solid concrete!'

'Well, I'm . . . flabbergasted!' Mr Butch said.

They continued to stare all around the room. Eventually they even looked up at the ceiling. If they'd done that as soon as they'd walked in they might have got a clue to how Danny and Josh escaped. They might have seen a sleek leopard-skinned gecko and a shiny pink gecko dart across the suspended tiles.

But by the time they'd even thought to look up, Josh and Danny had long since run down the wall and out through the top corner of the open door.

'Who-hoooo! Score! Ten-nil to US!' cheered Danny as they ran speedily along the ceiling of the store, skittering around light fittings and suspended signs with great ease. It was a fabulous ceiling to walk on—smooth and white, with enough obstacles to be fun. He didn't even mind that he was still pink and Josh had got to be the cool leopard-skinned version again.

'Head for the door,' called Josh, 'We'd better get outside before we change back. We don't want to drop from this height when we SWITCH back into boyaaaaaaaaaagh!'

At this point, Josh SWITCHed back. Two seconds later Danny did the same.

They both plummeted to the floor.

Here Be Dragons

The ceiling was high. A good three metres higher than in a normal house. And beneath it lay sparkly white tiles laid over a solid concrete floor. Had Josh and Danny been a metre off to one side they would have smacked onto the unforgiving tiles and most likely have broken several bones.

Happily, they had been scurrying across the ceiling just above the FLUMPYWUMPY display. A round, shallow plastic container, rather like a large paddling pool stood up on six sturdy legs at table height. It was filled with hundreds of Flumpywumpies . . . strange fluff filled glittery creatures which were all the rage among girls at school right now. If you pulled a string on a Flumpywumpy's back it would gurgle: 'Flumpywumpy wuvvs you!'

Danny and Josh hit the Flumpywumpies at great velocity, sending a shower of them into the air and over the edge of the display. Several of them told Josh and Danny they 'wuvved' them—in spite of the crushing and the throwing.

'Quick!' Josh hissed, scrambling through a multicoloured cascade of Flumpwumpies and onto the floor. But as soon as he spoke he knew something was wrong. His voice was all high and chirrupy—and his vision was astoundingly good—he could see all the detail of the My Tiny Horseys, half an aisle away. 'Uh-oh!' he said, turning round to look at Danny. Danny was brushing several Flumpywumpies off his jeans and kicking more back under the display. Right up to his waist he was back to normal. But above his waist he was still a gecko. Boy sized but with gecko arms, hands and fingers, a gecko chest and a gecko head covered in gleaming scales of shiny pink, with two bulbous, orb-like dark eyes.

Danny turned and saw Josh a second later. 'Oops,' he squeaked. He glanced into a mirror in the nearby Barbie display and then over to Josh again, feeling panic rise in his chest. 'We've got to get out of here!'

There was a lot of noise over by the exit. Far, far too many people were around. Loads of little girls in sparkly frocks and tiaras were piling through the doors. Oh no, remember Danny. The Damsels Party! But worse, away to their left, Danny could now see the security guard stalking along the top row of toy aisles, looking left and right, obviously searching for him and Danny. He might just recognise their jeans and trainers! 'We're just going to have to make a run for it!' he squawked at his brother, and the pair of them set off, pelting along the aisle and making for the doors.

They expected screaming. A lot of it. Danny was hoping the fear and horror would mean the girls would just run away as they approached, clearing their path to the outside world. And true—there was a lot of squealing as they ran up to the doorway—but not the kind they expected. There were about 15 or 16 girls and half a dozen mums with them, along with a Princessland Entertainer, dressed as a court jester, waving a stick with bells on and being determinedly jolly. And as soon as the girls and their mums saw Josh

and Danny, both still half-boy-half-gecko, they
squealed . . . with DELIGHT!

'Dragons! Oh look! They've got us DRAGONS!'
squealed the damsels. And they fell upon Josh
and Danny as if they were a basket of free Diddly
DeeDees, giggling and cooing and stroking their
heads.

'Amazing costumes!' one of the mums said. 'So
lifelike!'

Josh and Danny were appalled. They were surrounded by a crowd of damsels who were now pulling at their arms and dragging them across to the party area. This was a space right in the middle of Princessland, with lots of little glittery chairs laid out in a circle. Inside the circle was an assortment of girly fun—a large dolls' house, a small fabric tent shaped like a pink castle, dozens of My Tiny Horseys pulling along pumpkin shaped coaches with princess dolls in them, a hair braiding table, a bracelet making corner and a face painting stand . . . all laid out for a party.

'Wait!' called a shrill voice. 'I know what we're going to do!' It was a girl with curly red hair, topped with a silver tiara, wearing a white frock with pink roses stitched all over it.

'Melissa sweetheart!' cooed her mum, just behind her. 'We're going to make bracelets and have face painting and hair braiding.'

'NO!' shouted Melissa. 'It's MY party and I say we have a dragon FIGHT!'

The rest of the girls whooped with excitement.

'And this is MY dragon!' Melissa threw her arms around Danny. 'Because he's PINK! And that's my favourite colour! Who's on my PINK dragon side?!'

Several girls shrieked with approval and got behind Melissa, ready to cheer on the pink dragon.

Another girl with long dark hair and a red dress claimed Josh. 'OK—I'll have the spotty dragon!' she sang—and the rest of the girls ran to be on her side.

'My team against Lucy's team!' declared
Melissa, as the Princessland entertainer and the
mums stood by helplessly. 'Our dragons will
FIGHT TO THE DEATH!'

Josh and Danny stared at her. They were in
Princessland, standing in between two crowds of
damsels—and the damsels, with their rosebud
dresses and tiaras and shiny ballet shoes . . .
wanted them to FIGHT TO THE DEATH?! Danny
felt a grudging admiration rise through him. These
girls weren't all bad, he decided.

'Darling . . . that seems a bit . . . violent,'
simpered Melissa's mother.

'Yes, it DOES, doesn't it?' Melissa picked up a
long baton from a nearby majorettes twirling sticks
display. 'Here you are, *Pink* Dragon! Go beat up
the spotty dragon!'

A high pitched roar of approval went up,
drowning out the Princessland entertainer's
protest, and then the dark haired girl seized
another twirling baton and handed it to Josh.
'Bash his brains in, Spotty Dragon!' she urged. The
batons were long silvery sticks with heavy sparkly

balls on either end. As Josh and Danny took one
each they realized these could actually do quite a
bit of damage.

'We've got to get out of here!' hissed Josh,
glancing all around for an escape route. But they
were surrounded by girls—many of them linking
arms as they stood whooping and cheering.

'FIGHT! FIGHT! FIGHT! FIGHT!' goaded
Melissa.

'Ah come on,' grinned Danny, gripping his
baton and holding it out between both reptilian
fists. 'We might as well give them a show . . .'

To the Death!

'TO THE DEATH!!!' Danny shrieked as he ran at
Josh, holding the baton like a mace. It came out a
bit high pitched and chirrupy.

Josh sighed and sidestepped his brother at the
last second but Danny was expecting that and he
swooped his baton to the left, whacking Josh in
the middle of his scaly chest. There was a roar of
approval from Melissa's team.

'Gah! Right! You ASKED for it!' squeaked Josh,
spinning around and bringing his own baton up
to whack Danny on the arm. Lucy's team gave a
shrill cry of approval and started chanting 'FIGHT!
FIGHT! FIGHT! FIGHT!'

Danny let off an angry chirp as the heavy
rounded end of Josh's baton connected with his
elbow—and he swung his baton around and

thwacked his brother on the ribs.

Then Josh got really angry and bit him. Hard.
On the shoulder.

'Yeeeow!' screeched Danny. 'That's dirty
fighting!'

'Oh yeah?!' grinned Josh, leaping from left to
right as his brother tried to land another baton
thump on him. 'So what are you going to do
about it, Pinkie?!'

Danny let out a cry of rage and threw himself
on Josh, snapping his sharp teeth down hard on
the back of Josh's neck. Around them the damsels
were in a frenzy of cheering and chanting and
the mums were now trying to shout them down.
The Princessland entertainer was waving his little
jester's stick around and calling for calm.

Josh shook Danny off and then jumped onto
his brother's chest and snapped his own sharp
teeth on Danny's shoulder. A moment later they
were rolling across the party circle floor, knocking
over the friendship bracelets stand and sending an
avalanche of beads across the tiles.

Josh and Danny were having the time of their lives. They had never fought like this before. They'd scrapped often enough, of course—they were brothers—but a really full on FIGHT like this? Never!

If Josh hadn't spotted the security guard and the store manager running towards the cacophony things might have got more serious. But seeing Mr Butch and the square faced guard helped him to remember who he was. And who Danny was and what they had been trying to do when they got caught up in the Damsels' Party. ESCAPE! That's what!

Josh rolled into the pink castle-shaped tent, dragging Danny with him, and, hoping desperately that he wasn't about to make things even worse. Out of sight of the baying damsels, he pulled the SWITCH spray out of his pocket for the third time and squirted a bit at Danny and then himself.

Outside, the security guard was already pushing through all the screaming damsels and making for the doorway to the pink tent castle. He looked furious. He'd had more strife in one afternoon in Princessland than he'd ever had working with young offenders . . .

But then he slid on a slick of friendship bracelet beads and shot across the floor, cannoning into the face paint stand. A large pot landed on his nose, daubing him with glittery yellow. All the damsels burst into fits of uncontrollable giggling.

He struggled up onto his knees and crawled towards the tent, growling with fury. But when he tore open the curtains at the tent doorway he was once again confronted with nothing. Nobody there at all!

'What is GOING ON?!!' he wailed, sinking back down to the floor. 'I've been working too hard,' he told himself as his forehead thumped onto the floor. An orange flumpywumpy slid down his face. 'I wuvv you!' it told him. He didn't notice the leopard-skin and pink geckos shimmying up over his shoulder and shooting out of the castle tent window.

There was a pillar near to the pink castle. In fact, the structure had been tied up against it for extra stability. Danny and Josh shot up the pillar so fast they were nothing more than a blur to anyone watching—and nobody was watching. They were far too interested in seeing whether the big security guard was going to stop crying and come back out of the pink castle.

In the Bag

Danny and Josh got outside the store in less than
a minute and then shot into some shrubs which
grew alongside it. They sat, motionless, waiting to
SWITCH back again. For several minutes they said
nothing. Danny licked his eyeballs once or twice but
other than that they just kept still.

Finally Danny spoke. 'That was . . . kind of weird.'
The scales on his shoulder were sore and bruised,
even though he'd SWITCHed back down to gecko
size. The back of Josh's neck was also covered in
teeth marks. 'Sorry, Josh. I really didn't mean to bite
you that hard.'

'Yes you did,' Josh said. 'But so did I. Don't feel
too bad—we couldn't help it.'

'What do you mean?' Danny asked. He was
feeling very guilty about the great glee with which
he had attacked his twin just ten minutes ago.

'We're both geckos and we're both male,'
explained Josh. 'Female geckos can get along fine
together but male geckos can't. They're really
territorial and they quite often fight to the death.'

Danny gulped.

'It's just as well that security guard came along,'
Josh said. 'I might've bitten your head off.'

Danny smirked. 'I'd like to see you try . . .'

'DON'T!' Josh waved his gecko hand at Danny. 'Seriously! DON'T! We mustn't let that happen again. How will I explain it to Mum? She'll ask where are you and I'll have to say I bit your head off. She won't like it, you know.'

'She'll be fine—because I will have bitten YOUR head off!' snarled Danny, getting up onto all four feet and baring his teeth.

FFFFFFFFOOOFFF!

And then he was crouched on his hands and knees with his head poking up out of the bushes, still baring his teeth—and Josh was doing the same. Fortunately they were both boy shaped again. Completely, this time.

'Phew!' sighed Josh. 'That was close. Come on—let's go home. I've had enough excitement for one day.'

Danny nodded, getting up onto his feet and looking around, embarrassed.

They dusted themselves off, noticing that there was still a bit of blood on their boy skin and some little bite marks. Then they set out for home.

'WAIT!'

They froze, getting ready to run. Someone was skipping out of Princessland after them.

'WAIT!'

It was Melissa, waving two party bags. 'The lady in Princessland said you two were our dragons!' she puffed, as she reached them. 'You were so COOL! She said you must have these spare party bags. Here you go! Thanks for the fight!'

And then she was gone, leaving them with the bags.

Danny and Josh turned and ran.

When they got home they sank gratefully onto the grass in their front garden. Danny started foraging through his party bag. 'Cake!' he announced, pulling out a large golden wedge of sponge, topped with thick pink icing. Josh found one too and they both stuffed the cake at high speed, super hungry after all the excitement.

'What else?' murmured Danny, digging into the bag again. 'Bracelet—eurgh!' He chucked a stretchy bead bracelet onto the grass. 'Diddly DeeDee! Oh no! I never want to see another Diddly DeeDee!' He chucked that on top of the bracelet. 'Jelly beans! Woohoo! Kazoo . . . not bad. And . . .' Then he stopped, puzzled. At the bottom of the bag was a bit of screwed up notepaper.

'Jo-osh . . .' he said.

Josh had been going through his bag too, finding all the same things . . . and now . . . he too had some screwed up paper.

What made them both go very quiet and still was the familiar spiky writing. They opened out the notes and saw they were exactly the same. Each read:

HELLO AGAIN, JOSH AND DANNY.
AMAZING ESCAPE!
YOU ARE BOTH SO WORTHY
OF THE DESTINY WHICH
AWAITS YOU . . .
DARE YOU SEEK IT?

Danny gulped and stared at Josh. 'The Mystery Marble Sender!' he whispered. 'They must have been right there in Princessland—watching us!'

'I know,' breathed Josh, glancing all around them. 'They could be here now!' He shivered.

They read the next bit of their notes. The bit that always came next . . . The clue.

DON'T BLOW OR SUCK—HUM IF YOU CAN.
AND IF YOU CAN'T—YOU WIN!

'What?' Danny stared at the note. 'What kind of a clue is that?'

But Josh was smiling. 'An easy one. Which is just as well because I'm not doing anything else good. No more adventures! I need a cup of tea and a nice sit down!'

'You've just turned into your own granny,' observed Danny. But he knew what Josh meant. They needed a break from weirdness for a while.

Josh picked up both the kazoos. 'Here you go,' he said, handing one to Danny. It was a good quality one, chunky and made of metal. 'Blow in it and it won't work. Sucking on it won't work either.'

'No! You have to hum!' cried Danny and he stuck the kazoo in his mouth, closed his lips around it and hummed a little tune. It came out as a lively buzz.

'You can hum,' Josh said. 'So you don't win. Now let's see . . .'

He put the other kazoo to his lips and started humming. Nothing came out except a dull murmur. No buzzing. No humming. Josh grinned at Danny. 'I win,' he said.

And he tugged at the little round porthole style window on the top of the metal barrel until it came off. Underneath this should have been a fine film of tissue paper, but instead he found something small and round. A lump of glass.

He tipped it onto his palm.

One perfect glass marble, with a ribbon of colour running through it. Getting out his magnifying glass, Josh could just make out the code inside—and the hologram of what looked like . . . a whale. 'Yup—it's another SWITCH marble,' he confirmed. 'But I think this one must be for you,' he chuckled, handing it to Danny.

'Oh very funny,' Danny said.

The marble was pink.

DIARY ENTRY 701.2

SUBJECT: NEW HOME

What a relief to finally have the new laboratory set up! And it was good that Josh and Danny managed to follow my instructions and get in here so easily after SWITCHing into geckos. Very handy spray, that! They're much less vulnerable as reptiles than they would be as insects—and they can walk up walls and along ceilings and through cracks. They'd make excellent burglars or spies . . . now that is a thought for the future.

The only problem is the on-going instability of REPTOSWITCH. I really must get to the bottom of it because it's the second time a lizard SWITCH has gone a little off kilter. And of course the Amphibian one was problematic too, and the two species are very closely related. I must find out what's going wrong.

Mind you, Josh and Danny seemed to be fine today and obviously got home again unscathed and without further incident. I'm probably worrying too much!

Meanwhile I must also study the SWITCH marbles and the notes which came with them to try to discover who this Mystery Marble Sender is. It is most disquieting! Could it be Victor Crouch, alive and well after all this time, trying to mess with my genius mind? But why? If he had stolen my code for MAMMALSWITCH surely he would just claim it as his own—wouldn't he?

Something about those notes keeps bothering me . . . Dare you seek your Destiny? It says that every time. But why? There is something very familiar about that sentence . . . I MUST remember! I MUST! I MUST!

I will now go and hit the back of my skull repeatedly with a frying pan. Sometimes that works. Better find a clean one, though. Last time I remembered three things—but had scrambled egg stuck in my hair for a week . . .

GLOSSARY

Amphibian—An animal that can live on land and in water.

Antidote—Something which takes away the bad effects of a poison or disease.

Arachnid—A member of the group of animals that includes spiders and scorpions.

Cellular—Made from cells.

Hijack—To take control of something by force.

Hologram—A type of photograph made by laser beams, that appears to have depth as well as height and width.

Laboratory—A room or building equipped for scientific work.

Mammal—Any animal of which the female gives birth to live young and can feed them with her own milk.

Pigment—A substance that colours something.

Prosecute—To prosecute someone is to make them go to a lawcourt to be tried for a crime.

Reptile—A cold-blooded animal that creeps or crawls. Lizards and snakes are reptiles.

Scales—The thin, overlapping parts on the outside of fish, snakes, and other animals.

Serum—A kind of fluid used in science and for medical purposes.

Setae—Setae on gecko footpads are small hair-like pads responsible for the animal's ability to cling to vertical surfaces.

Snout—The front part sticking out from an animal's head, with its nose and mouth.

Territorial—A territorial animal guards and is defensive of an area of land it believes to be its own.

Transparent—Something is transparent when you can see through it.

PLACES TO VISIT

Want to brush up on your reptile knowledge?
Here's a list of places with special areas dedicated
to our scaly friends.

New Forest Reptile Centre
http://www.new-forest-national-park.com/new-forest-reptile-centre.html/

London Zoo
http://www.zsl.org/zsl-london-zoo/

Chester Zoo
http://www.chesterzoo.org/animals/reptiles/

WEBSITES

Find out more about nature and wildlife using the
websites below.

http://www.nhm.ac.uk/kids-only/

http://kids.nationalgeographic.com/

http://www.switch-books.co.uk/

http://www.arc-trust.org/

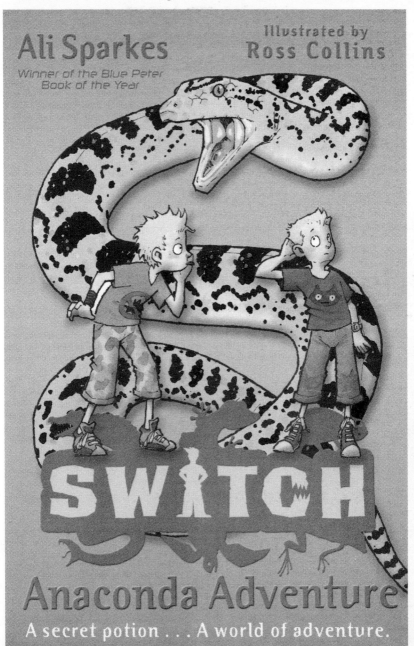

Another exciting adventure awaits . . .

Ali Sparkes
Winner of the Blue Peter
Book of the Year

Illustrated by
Ross Collins

SWITCH

Anaconda Adventure

A secret potion . . . A world of adventure.

Getting Legless

'Slithery, slithery, slithery . . . ' Petty Potts
pushed her face up against the glass, steaming
it up with her breath and bending her nose
sideways.

'She's going wrong again,' muttered Danny.

'Ahem! Who's *she*?' demanded Petty Potts,
stepping away from the glass and shoving her
thick spectacles up the bridge of her nose so
she could glare at him. 'The cat's mother? I was
merely trying to build the excitement.'

'You don't need to build any excitement!'
Josh pointed to the enormous snake on the
other side of the glass. 'You're just about to
SWITCH me and Danny into one of *those*. It
doesn't get more exciting than that!'

'Although we're not sure why you want

to do it *here*,' Danny added. They were in the reptile house at The Wilderness Zoological Park. 'I mean—surely it would be safer to do this SWITCH in the lab?'

'It would,' Petty said. 'But I'm working on a new theory. Will your behaviour patterns be affected if you SWITCH in close proximity to a real snake?'

Josh and Danny stared through the glass and shivered with excitement . . . and a little fear. On the far side a yellow and black scaly face rose up, staring back at them through almond shaped eyes. A black forked tongue waved in the air, trying to scent them.

'A yellow anaconda,' read Danny, peering at the little information plaque next to the display. 'Grows up to two or three metres in length and eats birds, reptiles and mammals. Non venomous. Kills prey by constriction. Not large enough to kill humans. Aaaw!' He turned to Petty. 'I want to be large enough to kill humans! Why can't I be large enough to kill humans? It's not fair.'

Josh thwacked the back of his twin brother's head with a rolled up Wilderness Zoological Park souvenir guide, briefly flattening Danny's spiky blond hair. 'You're not planning to kill any humans, are you? So it's not really a problem!'

'I know . . . ' pouted Danny. 'I'd just like to know we could if we wanted to . . . '

'Which is precisely why you're getting this SWITCH spray,' Petty said, holding out a small white plastic bottle with a spray nozzle on the top. The letters 'Y A' for yellow anaconda were written on it in permanent marker. 'I do have a green anaconda spray too, and they're the huge, human-eating size. But that's for later. For now, I don't want you getting over-excited and deciding to crush me to death on a whim. And in any case, you're only going to be SWITCHed for half a minute. This bottle has a very precise spray button and I've calculated the dose for exactly thirty seconds and no more.'

When Josh and Danny had first been SWITCHed it was by accident—into house spiders. It had been utterly terrifying to be the unwitting guinea pigs for Petty's Serum Which Instigates Total Cellular Hijack—and it would never have happened at all if Piddle, their dog, (named after a rather unfortunate habit he had when he got excited) hadn't run into their neighbour's back garden. It was while rescuing him that they'd stumbled into Petty's secret underground laboratory—and right into a jet spray of SWITCH.

Now, months later, it was hard to imagine how they'd resisted getting involved with Petty's SWITCH Project. Since they'd helped her find the missing code to the Reptile SWITCH formula they'd been more and more excited about taking part in the experiments. Being SWITCHed into reptiles was going to be amazing!

Even so, today Josh felt a twinge of worry—a zoological park was a bit public for a brand new SWITCH. 'Are you sure about this?' he asked Petty. 'It will definitely only last thirty seconds?'

'Certain!' Petty said. 'Now—check there's nobody coming and we'll give it a blast.' While Josh and Danny poked their heads out past the door of the reptile house—a humid hexagonal building filled with large glass-fronted displays containing all kinds of exotic cold-blooded creatures—Petty put her bag down on a table in the centre of the room. It was used as an education centre too, so there were tables and chairs and benches along one wall.

'Nope—nobody around,' Danny said, coming back in. 'Good job we're off school on a teacher training day. This place would be full of kids at the weekend.'

'Yes—but school parties sometimes come in too,' Petty said. 'And I saw one back by the entrance gate. Still—if nobody was anywhere near the bottom of the path we know we have a minute or more. It's a long walk up here. So—climb on

the table please. As soon as you SWITCH, pay
attention to the yellow anaconda. Look at it. And
let it look at you. I will be filming to see if there are
any differences in behaviour. And you'll SWITCH
back in half a minute—so no chance to get
chummy with my windpipe!'

Danny and Josh sat cross-legged on the table,
grinning with excitement. They'd been looking
forward to this moment for weeks and weeks—
ever since they'd found the last REPTOSWITCH
cube and Petty had begun working on the new
formula. Josh decided to stop worrying and just
have fun. He fixed his blue eyes on Petty and said
'Ready!' Petty sprayed him in one short burst.
Then Danny.

Three seconds later two yellow anacondas were coiling on the table, black and yellow scales gleaming in the soft light, diamond shaped heads swaying back and forth and black forked tongues flickering in the air.

'YESSSSSSSSSSSSS!' hissed Danny.

'This is SSSSSSSSSSO cool!' hissed Josh.

Although it was weird to have no arms or legs, he could feel the immense strength and agility of his sleek body. He lifted his head, feeling the muscles contract and relax in waves just under his beautiful gleaming scales, and rose up majestically to stare at Danny.

'Look at my toooongue!' Danny poked out his forked tongue and waved it around. It was like a tiny snake in itself—strong and agile.

'We're quite small,' Josh said, eyeing his tail. 'About a metre, I think. Not big enough to kill much more than a mouse. Oooh—quick—look at whatsisface! We've only got about ten seconds left.'

Whatsisface, the real anaconda, was now staring at them through the glass with interest.

He'd risen up higher and his tongue was going crazy . . . but he couldn't hope to get much information through it, thought Josh. Not with that thick glass between him and them. Petty's experiment would have worked better if he and Danny had been able to get in with the other snakes, behind the glass. But as anacondas occasionally ate each other, it was probably just as well they hadn't.

'How are we talking this time?' asked Danny, writhing around in great excitement, his scales rubbing together with a soft whispery noise.

'Oh—like most reptiles—through scent and body language and a bit of hissing,' explained Josh. 'You're smelling through your tongue!' Josh was mad about wildlife and knew a lot of this stuff. 'Ooh—I can't wait to do this back in Petty's garden. We can go into the stream at the back. You know anacondas are brilliant swimmers, don't you? They spend more time in water, in the wild, than on land!'

'Hmmm—but will she let us?' asked Danny. 'Since she's moved her secret lab to the attic above Princessland she's not doing any experiments in the old lab at home any more, is she? In case government spies are watching her!'

'Well . . . we'll just have to go off down the park and have a swim in the lake,' Josh said.

'Um . . . shouldn't we have SWITCHed back by now?' asked Danny. 'It's been more than thirty seconds, hasn't it?'

Josh turned to look at Petty and saw that she was legging it out of the room. 'WRONG SPRAY BOTTLE!' she shouted, as she went. 'GETTING ANTIDOTE FROM CAR! HIDE!' The last they saw of her was the back of her purple beanie hat—and even that looked quite panicky.

'Oh great!' Danny stared back at Josh. 'She's done a runner!'

'We'll be fine.' Josh gulped. 'She'll be back soon. We just have to hide in case anyone else comes in.'

The real anaconda was swaying about even higher now, behind the glass. Its eyes glimmered and its tongue was still dancing. It seemed to be laughing at them.

'Come on . . .' Josh said. 'Get down!'

They worked their way down the table legs, coiling around them to reach the floor. Under the table wasn't a good hiding place. They might easily be seen by someone walking in. 'This way!'

Danny hissed, sliding across the cold tiles and under one of the long wooden benches against one wall of the reptile house. Soon Josh and Danny were hiding in the shadows.

'She won't be long,' Josh said. 'She'll be back any minute. It'll be fine! Hey—I can feel her vibrations now.' And he *could* feel the vibration of steps back up the path outside. Of course, snakes were excellent at picking up vibrations— sometimes from far far away. Josh knew that it was one of the things which helped them hunt.

'Erm . . . isn't that quite a *lot* of vibrations for one genius scientist?' Danny queried.

And then the door crashed open and two dozen sets of feet pounded into the room.

And not one of them was Petty's.

FUN AND GAMES

There are more games for you to play and
download free on the SWITCH website.

www.switch-books.co.uk

Word search

Search for the hidden words listed below:

DANNY　　　　　SPRAY
JOSH　　　　　　GLADIATOR
PIDDLE　　　　　PRINCESS
PETTY　　　　　　DRAGON
GECKO　　　　　KAZOO
SWITCH　　　　　MARBLE

Y	T	T	E	P	Q	U	B	K	P
G	A	W	M	A	R	B	L	E	R
C	L	K	Z	E	J	O	S	H	I
D	R	A	G	O	N	D	T	V	N
E	B	Z	D	G	E	C	K	O	C
L	Q	O	A	I	P	F	U	G	E
D	V	O	N	Y	A	R	P	S	S
D	I	S	N	R	W	T	X	B	S
I	Y	B	Y	N	J	E	O	H	L
P	K	S	W	I	T	C	H	R	M

Answers on page 122

Spot the difference

These pictures *look* the same,
but can you spot ten differences?

Answers on page 122

True or false?

1. Some geckos can fly.

2. Reptiles warm up by sunbathing.

3. The smallest reptile is the mini-lizard.

4. The largest reptile is the mega-gecko.

5. Gecko's feet are really hairy.

6. Dinosaurs were reptiles.

7. There are about 100 different kinds of reptiles.

8. Geckos don't have eyelids.

9. Reptiles are bad parents.

10. Geckos can shed their tails.

Answers on page 125

Quiz

1. What has Petty Potts
been suffering from at the
beginning of the book?
a) A broken leg
b) Chickenpox
c) Cat mumps

2. What do Josh and
Danny find at 18 Rainbow
Business Park?
a) An extinct volcano
b) A disused water tower
c) Princessland

3. What kind of geckos
do Josh and Danny
SWITCH into?
a) Tokay geckos
b) Stump-toed geckos
c) Tree geckos

4. What does Danny
eat while he's a gecko?
a) Piddle
b) A spider
c) Josh

5. What's missing from
Victor Crouch's face?
a) Eyebrows
b) Lips
c) A nose

6. How do Josh and Danny
escape from the security
guard's office?
a) They climb out of the
window
b) They turn invisible
c) They SWITCH into geckos

7. Who's having a birthday
party at Princessland?
a) Petty
b) Melissa
c) Josh and Danny's sister,
Jenny

8. Where do Josh and
Danny find the pink marble?
a) In the security guard's
shoe
b) It's tied to Piddle's
collar
c) In a kazoo

Answers on page 123

Which SWITCH character are you?

Maze

Can you help Josh and Danny find their way out of Princessland and away from the security guard?

Answers on page 123

Answers

Word search (page 116)

Y	T	T	E	P	Q	U	B	K	P
G	A	W	M	A	R	B	L	E	R
C	L	K	Z	E	J	O	S	H	I
D	R	A	G	O	N	D	T	V	N
E	B	Z	D	G	E	C	K	O	C
L	Q	O	A	I	P	F	U	G	E
D	V	O	N	Y	A	R	P	S	S
D	I	S	N	R	W	T	X	B	S
I	Y	B	Y	N	J	E	O	H	L
P	K	S	W	I	T	C	H	R	M

Spot the difference (page 117)

Answers

Maze (page 121)

Quiz (page 119)
1.B, 2.C, 3.A, 4.B, 5.A, 6.C, 7.B, 8.C

Answers

True or false? (page 118)

1. False—although they're called flying geckos, they don't fly. Instead, they spread out their legs like a parachute and glide.

2. True—reptiles are cold-blooded so have to take their warmth from their surroundings.

3. False—the smallest reptile is the dwarf gecko—34mm long—as long as your little finger.

4. False—the largest reptile is the saltwater crocodile, which can grow up to 7 metres long.

5. True—their feet have pads on which are covered in millions of tiny hairs. This gives them amazing grip—even on glass.

6. True

7. False—there are about 7700 different kinds of reptiles!

8. True—they have a layer of membrane over their eyes which they lick to clean.

9. True—most reptiles leave their young to grown up on their own.

10. True—if a predator has got hold of a gecko's tail, it can shed it to escape.

About the author

Ali Sparkes grew up in the wilds of the New Forest, raised by sand lizards who taught her the secret language of reptiles and how to lick her own eyes.

At least, that's how Ali remembers it. Her parents, brother and two sisters argue that she grew up in a council house in Southampton, raised by her mum and dad, who taught her the not terribly secret language of English and wished she'd stop chewing her hair.

She once caught a slow worm and it flicked around like a mad thing and she was a bit scared and dropped it.

Ali still lives in Southampton, now with her husband and two teenage sons, and likes to hang out in the nearby Hawthorn Wildlife Centre spying on common lizards. The lizards are considering legal action ...

Whether you're interested in insects or revolted by reptiles, you'll love the SWITCH website!

Find out more about the creatures in Josh and Danny's adventures, enter fantastic competitions, read the first chapters of all of the SWITCH books, and enjoy lots of games and activities.

www.switch-books.co.uk